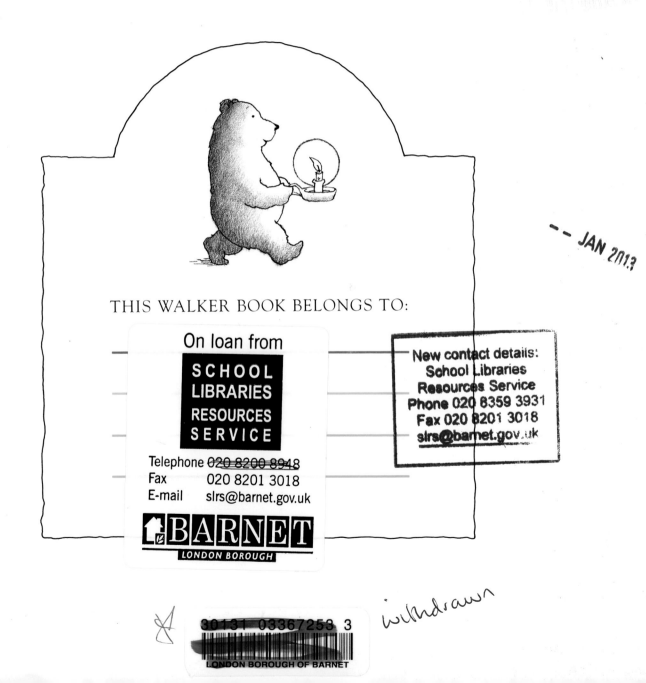

THIS WALKER BOOK BELONGS TO:

For Maria and Joe

First published 1991 by
Walker Books Ltd
87 Vauxhall Walk
London SE11 5HJ

This edition published 1998

2 4 6 8 10 9 7 5 3 1

© 1991, 1998 Catherine and Laurence Anholt

Printed in Hong Kong

British Library Cataloguing in Publication Data
A catalogue record for this book is
available from the British Library.

ISBN 0-7445-6189-2 (Hbk)
ISBN 0-7445-6070-5 (Pbk)

WHAT I LIKE

Catherine and Laurence Anholt

WALKER BOOKS

AND SUBSIDIARIES

LONDON · BOSTON · SYDNEY

What I like is…

time to play

a holiday

toys

(some) boys

waking early

hair all curly

What we like is...

jumping about

having a shout

going out

I don't like…

getting lost

I love...

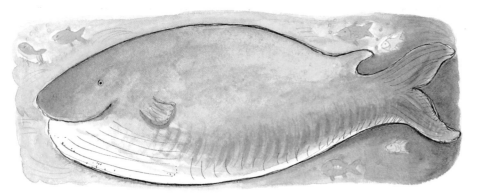 

whales and snails

dogs and frogs

lots of animals

Sometimes
we don't like...

being a pair

people who stare

having to share

I hate...

thunder and lightning

I like...

playing with my mother

and my new baby brother

What I like is...

ice-cream

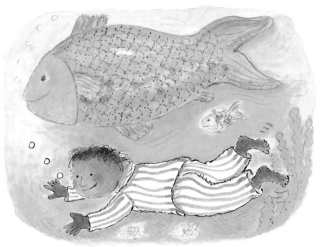

a funny dream

my thermos flask

my monster mask

I love...

playing the fool   a swimming pool   nursery school

I don't like…

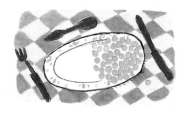 

fleas peas bees

aches snakes breaks

bumps lumps dumps

rats gnats bats

What we all like is...

a Christmas tree

watching TV

a place to hide

a pony ride

let's pretend

a happy end and . . .

Making a friend.

MORE WALKER PAPERBACKS
For You to Enjoy
Also by Catherine and Laurence Anholt

WHAT MAKES ME HAPPY?

"This lively picture book explores children's different emotions,
through their own eyes, using simple rhymes and evocative illustrations."
Mother and Baby

0-7445-6069-1   £4.99

KIDS

"From the absurd to the ridiculous, from the real to the imaginary, from the
nasty to the charming, this is a book which touches on the important aspects of life as
experienced by the young child." *Books for Keeps*

0-7445-6067-5   £4.99

HERE COME THE BABIES

"Over 70 warm and funny pictures of babies to amuse and entertain –
especially those with a younger brother or sister."
Practical Parenting

0-7445-6066-7   £4.99

Walker Paperbacks are available from most booksellers, or by post from B.B.C.S., P.O. Box 941, Hull, North Humberside HU1 3YQ

24 hour telephone credit card line 01482 224626

To order, send: Title, author, ISBN number and price for each book ordered, your full name and address,
cheque or postal order payable to BBCS for the total amount and allow the following for postage and packing:
UK and BFPO: £1.00 for the first book, and 50p for each additional book to a maximum of £3.50.
Overseas and Eire: £2.00 for the first book, £1.00 for the second and 50p for each additional book.
Prices and availability are subject to change without notice.